Clifford™
THE BIG LEAF PILE

Adapted by Josephine Page
Illustrated by Jim Durk

■SCHOLASTIC

From the television script
"Leaf of Absence" by Scott Guy

It was a beautiful autumn day on
Birdwell Island. Cleo, Clifford and T-Bone
were making leaf piles.

Cleo finished her pile of leaves.
They were red, yellow, orange, gold and brown.

She counted – one, two, three – and jumped in.

Clifford finished his pile of leaves.
They were red, yellow, orange, gold and brown.

He counted – one, two, three – and jumped in.

T-Bone's pile was not finished yet.
T-Bone's pile had only brown leaves.
Brown leaves make a nice loud sound.

"I need more leaves," T-Bone said.

"I'll help," said Clifford.

"I'll help, too," said Cleo.

And they did.

T-Bone's pile of leaves was ready.
But T-Bone had to go home.
It was time for him to go for a walk.

"I'll watch your leaves," said Clifford. "They will be safe with me. I promise."

"You're a good friend," said T-Bone.
And a happy T-Bone trotted off.

Clifford watched the pile of leaves.
He watched and watched some more.

"This is a very nice leaf pile," he said. "I can't wait to hear its loud sound."
"We could jump in carefully so we don't mess it up," said Cleo.

"Yes, we could," said Clifford.
"Then let's jump," said Cleo.

Cleo and Clifford ran to the pile and jumped in with a big *CRUNCH!*

The leaves flew.
A strong wind blew them everywhere.
"Oh, no!" said Clifford.

Clifford and Cleo chased T-Bone's leaves.
One leaf was on a weather vane.

Another leaf was under the mail truck.

Clifford and Cleo found a leaf on a swing in the playground.

They found a leaf on a plate of fries.

Clifford and Cleo found every one of the
missing leaves.

"This is a great leaf pile," said Clifford.
"I can't wait to hear the noise it makes,"
said Cleo.

"We could jump in," Clifford said.
"But we won't," they said together.

T-Bone came back.
His pile looked even bigger and better than before.

"Thank you for watching my leaves," he said to Clifford. "I want you to be the first to jump in."

"We must tell you the truth. We've already
jumped into your pile. All your leaves flew away,"
Clifford said. "But Cleo and I got them back.
I'm sorry, T-Bone."

"I'm glad you told me the truth," said T-Bone.
"I still want you to jump in first."

So Clifford jumped in with a big *CRUNCH!*

Then Cleo and T-Bone jumped in.
CRUNCH! CRUNCH!

And the three friends enjoyed the rest of the beautiful autumn day.

Other Clifford Storybooks:

The Big Egg Hunt

Camping Out

The Mysterious Missing Dog Food

The Runaway Rabbit

The Show-and-Tell Surprise

Tummy Trouble

Clifford is also available on CD-ROM.
Clifford makes learning BIG fun with these new CD-ROMs for children aged 4 to 6:

Clifford Reading
Clifford Thinking Adventures
Clifford Learning Activities

Scholastic Children's Books
Commonwealth House, 1-19 New Oxford Street, London WC1A 1NU
a division of Scholastic Ltd
London ~ New York ~ Toronto ~ Sydney ~ Auckland ~ Mexico City ~ New Delhi ~ Hong Kong

First published in the USA by Scholastic Inc., 2000
This edition first published in the UK by Scholastic Ltd, 2002

ISBN 0 439 98147 6

4 5 6 7 8 9 10 Printed in Italy by Amadeus S.p.A. – Rome